Star

A Modern Retelling of the Story of Esther
Valeria Saulsberry Edmonds

Table of Contents

Acknowledgements

I'd like to thank my friends and family for supporting my urge to be creative with my ministry. A special note of appreciation goes to my husband, Ricardo Sewell, who encouraged me to pursue my dream of publishing a book. I'd also like to thank my children for their honesty in critiquing my work and their patience while I spent quiet time reflecting on the messages in the bible that spoke to my heart as a woman and mother.

I want to acknowledge my tribe of women friends who stand behind me pushing, lift me up in prayer, and encourage me daily. There are many, but I'd like to express gratitude to a few in particular for their help with getting me over the finish line to publish this book and the other short stories I've written. I love you Robin McCoy, Anita Wolfe-Stewart, Elo Claire Odogbo, Valerie Adair, and Bonitta Saulsberry.

Preface

This story is for anyone who wants to dig into the challenges that we find in marriage today and understand a bit more about how to relate the story of Esther in the bible to our modern day challenges with divorce, dating and remarriage. I think we need to be able to see ourselves in the bible stories we read but often we can't because of the historical context. I see myself in the first wife who was displaced by Esther (no one ever preaches about her!) as well as in Esther, married to someone who has a different perspective on church and religion. It is my prayer that you find something in this story that speaks to you. There is always a little bit of me in herstory because I'm every woman...

Esther means "star."

Vashti and *Tiana* mean "beautiful."

Mordecai and *Marty* mean "warrior."

Chapter 1 - Clash of Egos

Most of the anger was gone. However, a year after the divorce, Xavier Thomas realized that he still missed quite a few things about his ex-wife, Tiana King. He had loved that his wife was extremely beautiful, with caramel-colored skin, large doe-eyes, and luscious lips. She was sexy and smart, which was a powerful combination in a woman. Together, they made a perfect couple; both were successful, well-educated and attractive. They enjoyed stimulating each other's minds and bodies.

Xavier was a great catch himself —handsome, well-dressed, and a successful CEO of his own construction company. Over six feet tall with an athletic build that was hard to hide in a suit, a close-cut fade, and delectable dark-chocolate skin; he was hard for women to resist. His marriage to Tiana had been one of his crowning personal achievements. He had grown up in the hood and scrapped his way through to survive and earn an engineering scholarship to

Georgia Tech. His perseverance and raw intellect had allowed him escape the cycle of poverty in his small hometown of Ft. Valley, GA outside of Atlanta. By marrying into her wealthy family, he had gained immediate access to social circles and political connections that would have been forever out of his reach otherwise. The guest list for their wedding had been a virtual who's who in black America as well as *Black Enterprise* 100 lists.

They were dubbed Nashville's most powerful duo when they were first married. He acquired a local construction company in her hometown after their engagement, then moved the headquarters of his thriving business from Atlanta to Nashville so that his bride could continue to progress in her career without having to move. Each had become even more successful with every passing year of their marriage. Tiana King was now vice president of marketing for her family's business, the largest black-owned bank in the South. She was pulling down a quarter of a million each year and calling the shots with their advertising campaigns in seven states. Xavier was doing equally well financially and was considered the king of construction. With her connections and his business acumen, his company was now one of the fastest-growing construction firms in the country. They had both become household names across the south by virtue of their careers and their likeability as a glamorous couple.

They were on top of the world and living the life most people only dreamed of with a beautiful home, luxury cars, and island vacations when they could fit them into their calendars. The two of them had plenty of money in the bank and enough investments to ensure they could maintain their lifestyle forever. However, the better they did professionally, the further apart they grew. They were too busy with their respective careers to even think about having children. Working long hours and traveling so often, they were like two ships passing in the night. Personal calendars and work calendars were so chockablock full that they had to schedule time to be together. More than once Tiana had told him, "If it's not on my calendar, it's not happening, babe!"

Tiana was very forthright and independent. She was a. take-charge and decisive manager at work, so it was hard for her to turn off the authoritative tone when she spoke to Xavier at home. He complained regularly that she didn't show him the respect he deserved as her husband, but she didn't see it that way. She believed they were partners and that they both should feel free to share their opinions. She saw no reason to placate his ego when she brought just as much to the table as he did.

Xavier knew she wasn't the "traditional" woman when they met. They could afford someone to cook, clean, and even shop for them, so she had long ago stopped doing anything that would have been close to "wifey responsibilities," and she didn't consult with him on anything before making a decision. They ran the house like a business. She was the COO, he was the CFO. Things ran very smoothly and they rarely had arguments.

They had a weekly date night, and the sex was pretty good—albeit unimaginative—when they could squeeze it into their schedules. Xavier worried that Tiana didn't look up to him because she had never told him she was proud of his accomplishments, which made him feel like crap. Hell, she never even took his surname. Sometimes he wondered why she had married him in the first place. He knew that he brought plenty to the table, but around her, he didn't feel important or even very accomplished. To appease his ego, he would occasionally sleep with one of the many women who were always throwing themselves at him. They definitely made him feel like a king. The other women that he spent time with always complimented his looks and oohed and ahhed when he spoke, as if he were saying something brilliant. Half the time, they didn't understand what he was talking about, but they would listen intently as he let off steam about problems at work. Xavier had never really had a serious affair; these dalliances were just sex. He loved his wife, but they had been going through the motions for years.

She noticed. Tiana didn't say anything to him, but she knew things were different. She could tell when he would rather stay longer on business trips than rush home to his wife. She could tell in his disinterest of things that mattered to her. She could tell in his half-hearted attempts to have conversation at dinner. She could tell when making love had become just sex. She didn't say anything to him. Yet she knew. Tiana cried when she was alone thinking that she deserved better. She stayed because indifference was better than being alone.

~

The Susa company banquet was the culmination of six months of fundraising activities through which Xavier's employees found creative ways to give back to the community. In Atlanta, the office had silent auctions and contests to raise money. While in Memphis, employees chose to participate in community events and log volunteer hours to see who did the most. The production facility in Nashville sponsored a large agency fair where non-profit organizations provided free services, carnival rides, and employees sold crafts to raise money.

A huge celebration was held to acknowledge all of the charitable giving the in the garden of a historic mansion in Nashville with managers from all 127 construction sites in attendance. It was an opportunity for Xavier to show off the profitability of business, so he typically invited potential investors, business partners, and city officials. That year the place was beautifully decorated for a winter wonderland theme with blue and white linen. The marble pillars had purple and white linen draped through silver rings, and couches of silver and gold sat on a mosaic pavement with marble, mother of pearl, and other costly stones. It was a much-awaited event each year because Xavier spared no expense with the entertainment or the food, and he ensured that the libations flowed freely. His employees, local dignitaries, and their guests danced the night away and had a great time.

As it happened, Tiana had scheduled a marketing conference the week of his Susa banquet that year. There was a big event the same night where she was the keynote speaker so she had not been able to make the banquet. He hadn't said anything to her but it did bother him that he was forced to go to the party stag. The guests didn't seem to notice. Everyone was happy because he had made it known that there was no compulsion to do anything but have fun. That's what he had decided to do as well.

He told himself. "Don't let it be said that Xavier Thomas doesn't know how to have a party!"

Late in the evening after the banquet was over, only his boys from home and his closest associates were left in attendance. Seven of his managers were with him as well and they had all fully utilized the open bar. They sat on various couches and chairs around the lounge area, waiting for the late-night entertainment that was always their favorite part of the event. The managers started to congratulate Xavier.

"Man, that was nice! Every year these banquets get better and better."

"Yeah, boss man, you outdid yourself this year. The turnout was off the chain, the food was great, and nobody stocks a bar like you do. I think I've polished off a whole bottle of Courvoisier by myself, and it was the expensive one too—the XO. Not that cheap stuff. Only top-shelf liquor for you!"

"It was beautiful too. You must have spent a fortune to get this place! I don't think I've seen this much gold and silver and crystal in my life. It looks like we were hosting the Academy Awards in here!"

Xavier was as buzzed as the rest of them. "It's a bit extravagant, but this is the one time every year we get to really celebrate. I look forward to having everyone dress up and party. We work hard and still find time to volunteer in the community. Tonight was my thank-you for all of your hard work, and I'm glad everyone had a good time. The only thing missing was my wife!"

His fraternity brother, Harold, was sloppy drunk and lying on a couch. His words slurred a bit as he joined in the conversation. "That's one fine woman you've got. You lucked out, dog, marrying money, brains, and sexy! Where wuzzzz Tiana tonight?"

Xavier took another drink straight from the bottle before

answering. "She had a work event tonight. It was an event that she planned and she scheduled it the same night of this banquet. I think she does that stuff on purpose! She should have been here by my side. She knows this is the biggest event of the year for my company."

Harold stood up and knocked over a chair. "Well, the after party is just starting. We've got a big suite upstairs and plenty of women up there. Give her a call and ask her to join us."

"Yeah, let me call Tiana and tell her to come over here! No need to have a party without the sexiest woman in town here. Especially since she's mine!" Still laughing, Xavier pulled out his cell phone and squinted to dial her number.

Tiana answered on the first ring, "Hi, Xavier. What do you need? It's late!"

"Baby, you missed a great banquet! I need you to come on over here and join the party. Me and the boys are still celebrating, and I want you to come too...but change into something sexy so that I can show you off. We're gonna play some slow jams and finish off the rest of this champagne. You love Cristal. I want to put my tongue in your ear—"

Tiana cut him off, speaking so loud into the phone that Xavier had to hold it away from his ear. "Boy, are you crazy! I'm not coming over there with you and your drunken friends! What do I look like coming after everything is over to dance with you like we're teenagers! The only place I'm going is to bed." She hung up and Xavier stood there looking at the phone.

The group of men had heard every word Tiana was yelling through the phone clearly, and one of them jumped to his aid saying, "That's okay, man! We can have a good time without her."

"Yeah, you know these modern women are too independent for their own good. Once they start getting a little authority at work, you can't tell them nothin!"

His friend Harold added, "You don't need her, Xavier. Man, she just disrespected you. Sometimes you have to put these women in their place. Show them 'who's the man'!"

Xavier collected himself. "I know, right? What ever happened to women standing by their man? Let's go see what those honeys look like upstairs. I bet they would appreciate this." He said pointing to himself. The others started talking and nodding their heads as they moved toward the elevator.

Meanwhile, Tiana was home thinking out loud while she prepared for bed. "I cannot believe that man. The nerve of him! Calling me drunk and asking me to come entertain him and his friends like I'm some floozy. When he gets home, I plan to give him a piece of my mind."

She lay in bed thinking about their marriage and wondering what more she could give. "Every time I think we're making progress, he does something stupid. He says I don't respect him, but then he acts like a child. I don't have time to stroke his ego! No one is stoking mine. I work just as hard as he does. If it wasn't for me and my family connections, where would he be anyway?"

She couldn't sleep. The more she thought about it, the more upset she became. "He knew that I was used to a certain lifestyle and goals before I met him. I need someone who can support my career too! There is no sin in being ambitious! I want to have it all—successful career, happy marriage, eventually children…but right now I'm focused on getting to be the president of the bank. Once I achieve that goal, then I can focus on the rest. I need for us to be equal partners in this marriage, but he thinks it should be all about him. He moved here for me, but that's water under the bridge. His company is doing well, and I'm proud of what he's accomplished. He needs to understand that I have my own goals! He'd better recognize! I'm not his little woman; I'm the best thing that ever happened to him."

~

Sitting off to the side of the room, Xavier watched as the other guys got their groove on with the various women he had invited to the after party from the Raven's Nest escort service. They provided several attractive and well dressed women for late night entertainment. Harold was the one person who suspected how unhappy he was at home. He had recommended the service as a way to distract Xavier from his troubles. The escort service catered to wealthy men and they were available for personal or group engagements.

Xavier poured himself another drink and called out, "I'll be right there, you guys. Save a bottle for me!"

Xavier was frustrated by how little influence he had in his own marriage. He sat there with the glass in his hand thinking that something had to be done about his wife's disrespect. When Harold came over a half-hour later, he found him still sitting in the same spot.

"What's up, man? You gonna join us?" Harold asked. "These girls are hot!"

"I'm so sick of Tiana and her big mouth. She doesn't show me any respect. Between her job, the sorority meetings, the Links, and other stuff, she never has time for me."

Xavier looked like he needed to vent so Harold didn't say anything.

"I can't remember the last time she cooked a meal or did anything around the house. She doesn't consult with me on anything before making a decision. In fact, she doesn't act like a wife at all. I really hate that she didn't take my last name. People are always calling me 'Mr. King' by mistake, like I latched onto her coattails to get to the top. Her contacts helped, but I built this company."

Harold finally chimed in. "That's what you get for marrying a career woman. My wife knows her place. That's why I married Daniella. I found a sweet little Dominican girl who thinks I'm wonderful. She cooks and cleans; makes sure that I'm comfortable when I get home from a long day at work. I don't ever have to worry about competing with her or her even questioning my judgement. Black women tend to be too sassy. When you cross one who is making her own cheese, it's even harder to keep them in check. Even you have said that before. You know your company was doing okay before you married her. Who's to say you wouldn't have made it this far without her family anyway? Black women need to learn how to appreciate a good man when they find one."

Xavier took a big drink from his glass. "Man you know

that's right! I was a great catch for her too! Sometimes I wonder what she thinks of me. I know that she's smart and her confidence is actually sexy, but every once in a while I want to be with someone who treats me like the man that I am. I could have any one of these women here if I wanted." The more he thought about it the angrier he got.

"Tiana has embarrassed me for the last time. She scheduled that event tonight although she knew this event was important to me; then she yells at me so loud on the phone that my employees could hear her. Well, I'm not taking this anymore. I don't need her, her connections, or this marriage. I'm going to party all night and forget all about her!"

"Exactly. Many let's go get this party really started!" Harold led the way.

~

It was no surprise that the fight that ensued between him and Tiana the next day escalated over the next few weeks. She tried unsuccessfully to discuss what happened. They had both invested a great deal into the marriage and she really wanted to make it work. It didn't matter that she hadn't been happy. Tiana knew that finding another man like Xavier would be difficult. Too many of her friends were single and the stories she heard about the creeps that they settled for to get an occasional night out scared her to death.

Xavier, on the other hand, had moved on. From the night of the party, he barely engaged her in any conversation. The fights were pretty much one sided with Tiana vacillating between having a fit about his behavior and trying to smooth things over. He finally completely shut Tiana out and refused to discuss options for reconciliation. He was done. Who needed a marriage that was more like a competition than a partnership? Tiana always had the last word and it bruised his ego that she didn't respect him as much as his managers at work. He shouldn't have to prove his manhood at home – he should the king of his castle. But he didn't tell her that. He just let her talk and decided she would figure it all out on her own since she was so smart. In the end, the only thing they agreed on was that it was over. The marriage had run its course and died a slow and painful death.

He insisted on a quick divorce and would not entertain any thoughts of marriage counseling. Because they didn't have kids and agreed to split everything fifty-fifty, the divorce went smoothly.

His divorce was final six months ago. Now Xavier was single again at thirty-five. He was open to marrying again, but he was a little gun-shy. He had struck out so badly with Tiana that his confidence in being able to choose wisely was lost. After a lot of soul searching, it dawned on him that his first marriage had been based on very superficial things like looks and status. Now he realized that marriage required much more to really work. He as in a better place now financially and he felt that he had a lot to offer a woman. He also believed that every man should be ruler over his own household and that a woman should be there to support her husband at all times. He didn't think that was too much to ask, but he knew it would be hard to find women who believed the same thing in this day and time. Women were too busy trying to "run the world," like Beyoncé.

Chapter 2 - Match Me

Xavier hadn't been on a real date in years. He didn't know where to look for a suitable partner. Where did respectable single women hang out? Online dating didn't appeal to him, and he was way past the club scene. There were plenty of women available for him if he just wanted sex but none that fit the bill for a potential wife of someone in his position or even to be his date in public. He still used the escort service occasionally but that was getting old.

Now it was time for the Susa Annual Charity Banquet, and as he sat there pondering his options for finding a date, his assistant came in. She asked the very thing he was thinking about.

"Who are you going to bring to the annual charity banquet this year? Everybody here is really looking forward to it."

Xavier smiled and said, "You must be reading my mind. It's hard to meet the right type of women. The women I've been with lately are only good for one thing. They're not the marrying kind…if you know what I mean."

"What you need is a nice church girl!"

"Whoa! Don't go there. All I need is someone preaching to me all the time. No scripture-quoting holy rollers for me. Thank you very much."

As he sat there looking puzzled, his assistant added, "Not every Christian is like that, you know. I have an idea. There may be a way to raise additional money for our cause while helping you get your swagger back at the same time."

Xavier raised an eyebrow. "Okay, you've piqued my curiosity. What are you thinking?"

"Let's ask each one of your department heads to bring an eligible bachelorette to the banquet. No one knows you like your management team. You can bet any girl who knows she might get a date with the most eligible bachelor in town would jump at the chance to catch you. We can auction off dances with you at the party. It will be like that *Who Wants to Marry a Millionaire* show but for charity."

"I think you're crazy, but what the heck. I don't have any other options and, who knows, I may just meet Mrs. Right. But don't make them pay to dance with me. There will be a silent auction and plenty of vendors there to get more money from the guests. I will provide every single woman who buys a ticket to the banquet a spa treatment at my club. The owner, Heather, will be able to screen them for me and steer me clear of any nuts that might show up."

Xavier smiled at the thought of getting matched up by his staff. He made a mental note to give his assistant a bigger bonus this year for being so creative. "Draft a memo for me to send to each of my department heads with the details as soon as possible. I think this may be the best banquet yet."

When Martin Kyle Johnson, head of production, received the memo from Mr. Thomas, he thought it was a joke. However, after hearing some of the other managers discuss what type of woman was right for Xavier in the cafeteria, he realized it was serious. Marty, as he was called, had never been to the annual charity banquets in the past because he knew that the folks at Susa Industries tended to drink too much and have wild parties. He had come up through the ranks and still associated mostly with the workers within the production department more so than the managers on the leadership team. Most of the folks in operations were from his part of town, and many had gone to school with him or his siblings. The people on the production floor were like family, and he understood them. Although he was on the management team, he wasn't really considered one of them, and he was fine with that.

Now that this new twist to the banquet had been added, Marty thought it might provide just the opportunity he needed to secure a good future for his young cousin, Esther, who he lovingly called Star. Marty had taken her in at eleven years old when her parents died, and he raised her like a daughter. He and Star were both active in church. He was head of the deacon board and she was the choir director. Although she was exceptionally beautiful, she seemed happy single with Jesus as her steady companion. At twenty-five, she rarely responded to the numerous invitations she got to go out. When she did go out, it never went beyond one or two dates with any one young man. All of her free time was spent at the church. After graduation from college she had gotten a good job at the bank, but she still lived in the house with Marty. He didn't mind, but he knew that her parents would have wanted her to settle down and have a family.

Although Marty didn't normally trust people with money, he didn't have any problems with Mr. Thomas. Xavier Thomas had supported his getting into management and left him alone to run his department the way he saw fit. The extra money from the promotion had made a big difference in their lifestyle, but he wanted more for Star. Marty wanted her to marry well because she deserved to be treated like a princess.

That evening, Marty decided to introduce the idea. After Star served dinner, Marty said grace then casually mentioned "I think we should go to the Annual Charity Banquet that they have for Susa employees this year."

Star look up from her meal with surprise. "That's funny. You never used to want to go to those company functions. What's going on?"

"Well the charity banquet is going to be a little different this year. There will be an opportunity for all the single ladies who attended to get free spa treatments and a dance with the CEO." Everybody in town had heard about his ugly divorce, but Marty figured he needed to tell her a bit more about Xavier to gage her interest. "You know I've worked for Xavier a long time and he's not only a good manager, he's a man of character. He supported me for my promotion and has always treated employees fairly. You can tell a lot about a man by how he makes business decisions.

Star, I truly think this is a great opportunity to meet someone who could take care of you for life. I know it sounds a bit like that show, *Who wants to marry a millionaire?* but Xavier is actually a respectable guy. I also understand from reliable sources that he really is looking for a potential wife. He doesn't have time to date so this is a way for the managers who know him well to do a little match making. There is no doubt that you would be the prettiest girl there, so let's go."

"It sounds like a highfalutin beauty pageant to me. Why would I want to go?" Star asked.

"Well, did I mention that it is for charity? You would be doing something for the community by purchasing a ticket and it would get you out of the house to meet more people. Think about it at least. It may be fun. I have a feeling that this might be a great opportunity for both of us. You said yourself that the types of men who ask you out don't have much conversation or class. Xavier might be just the type to stimulate your mind and introduce you to the world beyond this town. Just don't mention your relationship to me. There is enough cronyism in that place already. If he likes you, it shouldn't have anything to do with me or vice versa."

Star really didn't have a good excuse for not going. She would do anything for Marty given all that he had sacrificed for her. He was right in that eligible Christian single men with brains, good jobs, character and charm were hard to find. Not that they didn't exist, but after college, those that hadn't married right away had mostly moved away to larger metropolitan areas. The real reason she even considered going was that she found Xavier Thomas extremely attractive. She was impressed with his accomplishments and curious enough to want to know if he was as interesting a person as the press made him seem. Certainly having Marty's encouragement to meet him made this seem like providence.

"Okay I'll go. Just know that I'm doing this for you. I can't believe I'm agreeing to parade myself around at a party in front of your boss. Now I need to find something to wear!"

Marty offered to pay for a new gown and shoes. He wanted to make sure she looked like the princess she was as a child of God. They caught up on other aspects of their day and plans for the balance of the week. Star enjoyed listening to Marty's stories about the guys at work. She knew that he loved his job and that he truly cared about the people that worked for him. She had learned a lot from him over the years about leadership and the importance of building trust among your employees. He was well respected and well liked at work as well as in the community.

Although she didn't expect to, Star had fun getting ready for the big event, trying on dresses and shopping for just the right accessories. She felt a bit like Cinderella. She stopped at a different department store each day after work for a week until she found a dress that she thought was suitable. Everything she saw was either way too revealing or it looked like a 'mother-of-the-bride' dress. Star wanted to look her age, accentuate her assets and still leave something to the imagination.

Star hadn't been to a fancy dance since her prom night, and that had been a fiasco. Her prom date had only been the first of many who made her question where the godly men were in this world. Most of the guys she met were only interested in one thing and didn't even pretend to want to get to know who she was as a person. She longed for a man she could relate to intellectually, emotionally, and spiritually. Uncle Marty gave her hope that this type of man existed, but she believed that he was the last of a dying breed of men who knew how to maintain their manhood while allowing a woman to blossom and grow at their side.

The day before the big event she had an appointment at the spa to get her hair and nails done. When she arrived at the spa Star was greeted with the scent of lemongrass and soothing music that invited guests to take off their shoes and relax. She was more than slightly impressed by Xavier's health club and luxury spa, which was an oasis of serenity with a Thailand-inspired decor. The Zen atmosphere with seafoam-green walls and lush foliage made you forget immediately that you were nestled in the heart of the city.

"Good evening, Ms. Johnson. Welcome to Oasis Spa. As you know one spa treatment came as part of the event package. I see you've decided to get a spa manicure and pedicure treatment. This service includes a foot massage and paraffin wax. Here is a complete menu of other treatments. We do have some additional slots available if you want to take full advantage of your visit."

Star wished she could splurge on a massage and facial since she had never visited a spa but she felt blessed to be there. It wasn't the type of luxury that she could afford even on an infrequent basis. The salary she made at the bank was good but she had student loans to repay. She was also saving money to buy a new car because the used one her uncle had given her when she went to college was on its last leg.

.A gracious staff member offered her a thick Egyptian cotton robe and some ginger tea. "Help yourself to the sauna and steam room in this area. There is also a hot tub and steam shower this way. Maria is going to do your hair and the spa manicure and pedicure will be done in the same room. She will look for you in the relaxation room. You have an hour until your appointment and just relax. Let me know if I can get anything for you."

Star quickly changed out of her street clothes so that she could take advantage of the steam room and sauna. She had to cover her face with a cold wet towel so that she could breathe in the hot room but after some time in both her skin was glowing.

"So this is how the other half lives?" she said to herself as she relaxed in the meditation room with a water fountain covering an entire wall like art. The furnishings were luxurious and she almost fell asleep on one of the lounge chairs while waiting for her first treatment.

The owner, Heather, came to greet her and was instantly impressed by Star's fresh, unpainted beauty, and her modest demeanor. Star didn't come in demanding an upgrade to the most expensive treatments or talk to her like she was the hired help so that made her stand out from the crowd of women there as guests of Xavier. None of them knew that Heather was the owner, so it was easy for her to gather intelligence that she could feed back to him on who had potential and who did not. Star was very respectful and considerate of all the staff. Heather sensed that Star was special. Not only was she beautiful on the outside, she didn't appear at all vain. Heather decided to upgrade Star's spa treatments to include a facial, massage, mud bath and body scrub. She also added a complimentary lunch from the health club restaurant.

"Well, it looks like you will be with us most of the day." said Maria when she came to take her to the salon.

"Yes, this is really something. I've never experienced a whole day at the spa."

"Don't worry. We will take good care of you. It will be like escaping to another world and relaxation is good for the soul. The hair treatment will initiate the purifying process. The massage will improve blood circulation and releases serotonins which will make you feel good. The beauty treatments that you'll get will include a deep cleansing to make your skin come alive and all the essential beautifying oils. Water provides the yin and the yang – it gives you balance. So its good if you get a chance to get in the hot tub before the massage.

"Already did that. It was glorious to sit in the water and have the jets hit me." Star giggled. She was having so much fun. It was like she had died and gone to heaven. She said a quick prayer of thanksgiving then leaned back to let Maria do her magic.

After spending most of the day at the spa Star looked and felt like a movie star. Her body had a healthy glow and her skin was dewy fresh. Heather recommended a few products when she was checking out. They spent some time talking about the gala and the competition.

"I can't believe I'm participating in this crazy scheme of my cousin's boss to have his managers bring single women to a banquet for him to check them out. What type a man has a contest to find a date?"

Heather decided to give her a few insights on Marty's personality. "Well I've known him for some time. His first wife used to come here quite often and he has come to get massages himself. He's a really nice guy. I think he just spends too much time working to meet anyone and he's the type that actually likes being married. He asked me to screen the women who came for treatments to make sure he didn't get caught up with any nutcases. I think he's of the mind that if he gets one or two dates out of this, what the heck? He really doesn't have anything to lose but whoever he chooses could luck out. Heck, if I was single, I'd get in the running myself! He's attractive, rich, hardworking, educated and never been in jail. What else could anyone want?"

"Well that's not my criteria for a husband but it's not a bad list. I just want someone who is a Christian and serious about commitment. He definitely needs to be gainfully employed, but he doesn't have to be rich. If I'm blessed with someone who can hold a decent conversation and makes my heart skip a beat that would make him perfect."

"Humph! Girl, it won't hurt if he's rich too. I hope you enjoyed your visit today. We certainly enjoyed having you."

When Star left, Heather made a mental note to ensure she got one of the slots on Xavier's dance card the night of the banquet.

~

It was no surprise that attendance at the banquet was

higher than ever that year. Not only had his department heads made good on the "Match Me" challenge for Xavier, but it seemed everyone who was anybody in town had shown up as well. Xavier was busier than ever dancing with beautiful would-be partners and being introduced to women of all ages, races, and economic backgrounds. The rule was that once they had been introduced or danced, they could not monopolize his time and should not approach him unless he asked for them by name. That way, he could meet as many women as possible and be fair to all the ones who had shown up to meet him.

When the time came for Star to dance with Xavier, she remembered what Heather had told her about the type of women that he liked but she had decided to just be herself. Star looked fabulous. Not overdone like so many of the other women, with fake hair, fake nails, fake eyelashes, and fake infatuation. The gown she wore was a simple affair in black lace that had a high, round collar and three-quarter-length sleeves. The holes in the lace allowed just enough skin to show through to catch the eye. The underdress covered her bodice, followed her curves, and flowed with the lace into a cute little train at the back. Her hair was pulled away from her face into a crown of soft curls, and she wore just enough makeup to accentuate her beautiful brown eyes.

Star didn't talk too much or try to impress him with her accomplishments. When he spoke, she was attentive, and she only offered an opinion when asked. He was immediately attracted to her physical beauty, but he was even more surprised at how peaceful he felt in her company. There was something about her presence that made him comfortable and at ease. He danced with at least thirty women that evening, but it was no surprise that at the end of the evening, he asked for her by name. He sought her out and invited her out for a private dinner.

~

They went out the very next weekend and it was the beginning of a whirlwind romance. He showered her with gifts and was a complete gentleman to her. In her pleasant but serious manner, Star had insisted that he court her the old-fashioned way. Star was very clear that the purpose of dating was to get to know each other and that if a man decided to pursue you in earnest, then he had to be exclusive and intentional about a courtship with the goal of determining whether the other person was a suitable marriage partner.

Xavier learned her likes and dislikes, wined and dined her, and made love to her mind. He admired her faith and commitment to her God even though he wasn't really a practicing Christian. He didn't own a Bible and certainly didn't spend a lot of time in church before he started dating Star. He wanted to make love to her badly but respected her enough to wait. At this point in his life, he realized that a relationship had to be built on more than just sex and credentials. There was a light that emanated from Star that he was attracted to even more than her beauty. She made him want to be a better man.

Star was originally put off by the fact that he didn't attend church regularly. She told him that she could never be with someone who wasn't a Christian.

"I believe that a woman is supposed to submit to her husband as the head of the household. How could I knowingly commit to someone who was not following Christ? I want a husband who will lead me to heaven, not hell!" Star explained when he asked why it was so important to her.

"Well I am a Christian. I was raised in the church and I even went to a Catholic high school. It's just that I stopped going regularly when I left my parents' house. I was burnt out on church and it hasn't been a big deal since then. What difference does it make if I attend church or not? I pray every day and I am a good person."

"You're right in that going to church doesn't get you into heaven. However, I think that a man should be a leader in his home. That means I'm supposed to subject myself to his leadership. If I know that he's following Christ, then that makes me more comfortable following him. It's always been a deal breaker for me to be with someone who is a Christian."

That made sense to Xavier although he still didn't think

spending all your time in church was for him. From the time she mentioned that it was a deal breaker for her, he escorted her to church whenever she went. He even joined the male chorus and went to the men's ministry breakfast on the first Saturday of each month. They enjoyed each other's company and Star came to see for herself that he was not only a good leader at work, he was kind and generous and very attentive to her. He spent virtually all of his free time with her and even though it was a new experience for him, he never did more than kiss her. Star was still a virgin but he kissed her deeply enough to make her desire more. She hadn't expected to but she fell in love with him.

Xavier had originally been attracted by her beauty, but the more time he spent with Star he realized that it was her strength of character and her purity that really made her beautiful. He had never gone this long without having sex with a woman. Xavier asked her to marry him six months after they met, and even asked Marty for her hand in marriage. Star decided to fast and pray about her decision. Her biggest concern was whether they were 'equally yoked' but she was confident that he was a believer. She discussed it with Marty and her Pastor, and they both advised her to trust her heart. In the end, she truly felt that God had his hand in putting them together. He had turned out to have the full package – Christianity, charm, character, conversation, and even cash.

She had Xavier nervous when a week went by without an answer but he was as excited as a schoolboy when she finally said yes. He wanted a big wedding to show her off to the world, but at her insistence, they got married in a small private ceremony at her church with only twenty or so close friends. He decided not to invite anyone from work, other than Marty of course, because if he invited one, he'd have to invite hundreds As far as she was concerned the wedding was the beginning of their life together and the focus should be on the marriage versus the ceremony. Star walked down the aisle resplendent in a simple white satin and lace sleeveless gown with a v-neckline, mermaid silhouette, and a short train. She emerged as Mrs. Esther Starlette Thomas with the promise of

Xavier's commitment until death. At the reception, her cousin Marty toasted them saying "In John's second letter in the bible, he wrote to the chosen lady and said 'love each other and live in the truth.' That's what I want for both of you. I want you to walk according to God's commandments and abide in the teaching of Christ." As a twist, Xavier distributed gifts to all of the guests to celebrate his good fortune to have her as his bride.

Their life together was like a fairytale. Star moved into his mansion and quit her job at the bank. Marriage to Xavier was all she had dreamed. She had to adjust to having a maid to clean the house, landscapers to care for the property, a walk-in closet filled with designer clothes, and the primary responsibility of entertaining for her husband's business. Her life revolved around the church and her husband. Xavier was attentive and extremely pleased that she seemed to be satisfied not having a career outside the home. They both wanted kids and so she had decided to quit her job and focus on starting a family as soon as possible. A traditional marriage where he worked and she stayed home to manage the household suited them both just fine.

Chapter 3 – Malicious Intent

One night when Marty was working late he happened to come across incriminating evidence that revealed someone was embezzling funds from the company. As head of Production he was looking for some information on one of the companies listed in his operating expenses. He didn't remember actually using this particular vendor. A quick google search revealed that there was no company by that name either. As he sat their going over months of financial records it was clear that payments had been going to this company for over a year. He discovered that the CFO and one of the accountants had found a way to cook the books and move money into a bogus electrical lighting company.

Susa Industries was competing for a big contract at one of the new retail development sites in Nashville and this lighting company was listed as a subcontractor. If it went through, the accounting fraud would surely be discovered when they asked for financial records. Susa would lose thousands more and this would ruin the company's reputation. Xavier was also bidding on a huge construction project for the city to rebuild the city hall. He couldn't afford any scandal or mismanagement concerns right now. Marty knew that Xavier needed to be informed as soon as possible but he didn't know who to trust in the company. As far as he knew, other managers could be in on the scam. Instead of reporting what he found to security, Marty decided to tell Star. She was one person he knew they could trust.

When Marty told her what was going on, she did not take the threat lightly. Star prayed for her husband daily and something in her spirit had warned her to pray for his business recently. She also knew that if Marty had brought it to her, it must be very serious, because it wasn't in his nature to interfere or cause trouble. That evening when Xavier came home, he found his favorite meal waiting for him. Over dinner, Star told him about the fraud. She explained how Marty had found the accounting records and realized the company wasn't real. When Xavier's security team investigated the allegations, the two conspirators were fired. Marty's efforts were acknowledged in his employee file. However, Xavier's friend, George Hammond was head of security and he didn't like the fact that his team hadn't discovered this fraud. He also resented that Marty had gone around him to the CEO. George felt it made him look bad.

Chapter 4 - My Boy George

Shortly after the fraud incident, George Hammond was promoted to Executive Vice President with Susa Industries. Xavier and George had been classmates at Georgia Tech. The work relationship benefited from their personal relationship because they were great friends. George had gained Xavier's confidence even more as a business advisor and right hand man. The promotion demonstrated to all of the other managers that George was his favorite which caused some resentment.

When the announcement came out, it said that all the managers now needed to run everything through George. Marty was having a meeting with his section heads and made it clear that he was still running the production organization. He also said to the team "If necessary he could go straight to Xavier to make sure their plans for the year didn't get off track. I don't bow down to George Hamon!" He didn't trust George. Every time he tried to make process improvements or invest in new technology, George second guessed him in their management meetings. He wasn't sure what the issue was but George always found a way to try to make him look incompetent. He knew that this promotion was going to go to his head and he was on the offense.

A couple of guys that used to work for George were now in the Production Department. They reported back to George that Marty had shown him disrespect when the announcement came out. It was all George needed to get him fixated on ruining Marty's career. The fact that Marty was a Black man who had worked his way up the ranks to a senior position without any formal education bothered him but even he didn't know why Marty always made him so uncomfortable. There had always been an undercurrent of classism within the plant – a split between the local production workers and the headquarters personnel. The local town people worked mostly in production and felt like Xavier had brought in managers from outside into the highest paying jobs. Marty was the exception and George didn't think he should have a job on the leadership team because he didn't have a degree.

Marty represented the type of uneducated backward thinking people George hated. He didn't understand people who didn't bother to pursue higher education or travel and live outside of their home town. In his experience they were all too narrow minded and should be kept out of decision-making positions. He also didn't need anyone threatening his influence with Xavier. Marty was a do-gooder who was not shy about voicing his opinions of the cronyism he saw within the organization. He was always speaking on behalf of the workers and acting like a union rep. Marty was known for ignoring the political action committee requests to support political candidates that pushed favorable legislation for big business. George just didn't like him and wanted to find a way to get rid of him altogether.

George and Xavier were members of the same fraternity in college. They understood each other and had mutual admiration for the others' professional ambition. Xavier had been the only Black man in the organization but he was smarter than anyone George knew. Xavier was in a class by himself and George considered him exceptional for his race. He was indebted to him because Xavier had given him a job in management when he started Susa Construction. George was more than a little bit insecure because he didn't have any management experience before coming to work for Xavier. He had worked in retail sales after he graduated but he hadn't been thriving.

The job at Susa Construction had boosted George's income and his ego. He overcompensated for his lack of business acumen by going to conferences and making sure Xavier considered him a confidant on more than just matters of security. He sounded intelligent using a lot of business jargon and really believed he could run the whole company. He looked for every opportunity to weigh in on strategic decisions regarding the direction that Susa Industries should take. He had been involved in the decision to try lean production and open a manufacturing operation to build pre-fabricated and modular commercial building materials a few years back. More recently, they had been discussing ways to cut costs in the company, and George was trying to influence Xavier to move his production operations overseas, where they could get cheaper labor and building materials. Now with the promotion to Senior Vice President, he figured he could make it happen, and Marty and his whole department would be history. Xavier trusted him as a friend and listened to him when it came to business decisions.

"You can hire workers in China and India for a fraction of the wages you pay employees here in the US, and we could show a double-digit return on investment in as little as two years, even with severance costs." George was making another plea to shut down the production plants in the United States, and he was finally getting somewhere with Xavier, so he continued. "The workers that we have here are lazy, and they have gotten used to getting increases every year without any increase in production. These local folks don't think like us, man. They are not business people and don't understand that we need to do things differently to keep making profits.

We could keep chipping away at our operating costs here, but I'm telling you, we'd make a killing if we just moved the whole operation overseas. I'd be willing to forfeit my bonus this year to help defray the severance costs. That's how much I believe this is the right thing to do."

Xavier looked over the numbers George had put in front of him and nodded. "You're right. This would give us a twenty percent return in two years. I don't think we'll get that kind of cost savings in the next ten years with our current plans. You can keep your bonus, and you can handle the severance as you see fit. We need a solid change-management plan to make sure we can get it started within the next six months to make these numbers."

"I'm all over it. Just leave everything to me." George smiled as he left.

Within the next few weeks each department head was briefed on the plans for offshoring their operations. Marty was devastated when he heard the news. Not only did it have implications for him, but the production employees were locals who did not have a lot of other employment options in town. Xavier had acquired the local construction company ten years ago, but it had been a major employer in town for over seventy-five years. Losing these jobs would have a huge impact on the local economy and affect the livelihoods of hundreds of families.

Chapter 5 – Twinkle Twinkle

Marty was a praying man. He cried out loudly and bitterly at home that evening during his time with God. He decided to go into a period of fasting and praying until they found a solution and called on the deacons at his church to join him. Over the next week, the atmosphere at the company was very dismal, and many of the workers wore their pain visibly—particularly Marty, who grew sickeningly thin with concern for his people.

Star was extremely worried about Marty's health after she saw him at church the following Sunday. They hadn't seen each other in a couple of weeks which was unusual but she figured he was busy at work. After the service ended, she asked him what was going on and why he was so upset. Marty told her about the plans Hammond had put in place, including the details of the severance package and the schedule for when the transition would occur. Marty said he had known that Hammond was up to something, but he didn't think he would go this far. He urged her to speak to Xavier and try to get him to change his mind about the whole deal.

Star knew that she would be reaching beyond her place as his wife to get involved in Susa business decisions and she said as much to her cousin. "You know I don't have any authority to give him business advice. How do you propose I get him to change this decision when I don't even know the particulars? His friend, George, will make a fool of me if I try to interfere."

However, Star was truly concerned for her cousin. It seemed like Marty had aged ten years since she last saw him. He was really taking this decision to send the production work overseas badly, and she knew that something had to be done. They would need a miracle to counter the arguments for higher profits with saving people. In this day and age making money was supreme, and workers were just casualties of higher profits. Her husband was no exception to other businessmen who sometimes had to make tough decisions to satisfy shareholders.

Marty knew that Star was their only chance. Xavier wasn't a spiritual person, but he loved Star. The initial attraction might have been purely physical, but Marty had seen them together. Xavier was a different man when he was with Star. She bolstered his confidence with her admiration, and he worked really hard to make sure she was happy. Star brought out the best in him without even trying. She didn't know the power she had as a woman to influence a man, but it was time she found out.

He looked at her sternly and said, "Star, don't think that because you live in a big house, have a maid to clean for you and drive a fancy car that this doesn't affect you. That guy George doesn't care about any of us. He's just looking for a way to make himself look good. If you don't say anything, a lot of our friends and family members will suffer."

"But Marty, what can I do?"

"You are in a unique position of influence with Xavier, and I know that he will listen to you. But don't be confused. God is able! If you don't do anything, He will still provide.

You'll have to live with yourself, however, knowing that you might have made a difference. You and everything our family has ever believed in will mean nothing. Who knows? You may have been blessed with your position as Xavier's wife for just this purpose. Sometimes marriage is about ministry, not just companionship or sex or living well!"

Star thought about how blessed she was and how much she wanted to be used by God. She realized that she had a responsibility to others and that she couldn't live a selfish existence. She told Marty, "Ask the deacons and other leaders at the church to fast and pray for me. Tell them not to eat or drink for the next three days. I will fast as well, and then I will speak to Xavier. Even though it's not my place, I will make a case for the workers at Susa Industries, and if he decides to divorce me like he did his last wife for being disrespectful, so be it."

Chapter 6 - When a Man Loves a Woman

Star had been studying her husband and praying for him since their wedding. She knew what he liked and what bothered him. Star also knew that all the things that had attracted him to her in the beginning were still available for her to leverage. Star fasted and prayed for three days on the situation at hand. She prayed for God's direction on how to approach her husband with respect to the many jobs that would be lost.

On the third day she spent the morning at the spa making sure her skin glowed like the sun. Then she went to the salon to make sure her hair and nails were perfect. She put on her husband's favorite scent and her most flattering suit. By three o'clock in the afternoon, she was waiting in the reception area outside of his office looking regal and charming. Xavier was in his office, but she didn't interrupt. When his door opened and he saw her standing there, he broke into a wide grin and motioned for her to come in.

"Hi, babe! What a pleasant surprise!" Xavier said as she entered and gave him a quick kiss. "You look good enough to eat! What can I do for you, sweetheart? My queen! My woman! You know I'd give you the world."

"Sweetie, I didn't mean to disturb you. I just wondered if you'd mind us having a little dinner party tomorrow night. Nothing big. I was thinking we could invite your friend George and his wife, Zora. I want to do a little entertaining since we haven't had anyone over in a while." She had some events catered but if it was a small dinner party, Star enjoyed cooking herself.

"Is that it? Girl, you know I'd give you the moon if you asked. It's so rare that you ask for anything. Don't worry. I'll make sure the Hammonds are there. What time were you thinking?"

Star kissed him again but longer and deeper this time before saying, "Six would be great." She winked at him over her shoulder as she left and said seductively, "I'll see you tonight, honey! Thanks for everything."

Xavier sent George an e-mail telling him to bring his wife for dinner at six tomorrow and then got back to work. Seeing his wife in the middle of the day made him want to finish early so that he could get home and make love to her. Star was a wonderful wife. Attentive. Gracious. Sexy. They were in perfect sync at home. He knew he had won the wife lottery this time. It had been a while since Xavier had whistled while he worked, but all of a sudden, he was in a great mood.

The next night they hosted the Hammonds for a scrumptious feast of lobster tails and filet mignon. Star was a consummate hostess, and Xavier opened a bottle of his favorite Malbec wine from their collection. The table was set beautifully, with a simple bouquet of fresh flowers as a centerpiece. Candles glowed on the buffet. Soft jazz played on the house speakers. He was really proud to have her as his wife. She kept the conversation going and didn't let them talk about work. Star had even made his favorite dessert, a granny smith apple pie.

Their home was beautifully decorated with an art nouveau

décor but comfortable as well. Soft, simple furniture filled their rooms, and large picture windows were framed by light-colored walls and curtains. The hardwood floors shone to perfection, and the Austrian crystal chandelier in the dining room sparkled. They moved into the family room and sank into a large sectional sofa in front of the gas fireplace. As they were relaxing to the smooth sounds of Anthony Hamilton and sipping wine, Xavier repeated his question to Star. "Tell me something that I can do for you, sweetheart. You do so much to support me that I want you to have whatever your heart desires."

Star smiled and said, "Baby, you already do so much for me. You treat me like a queen, and I thank God for you every day. I had fun tonight. It's good seeing you relax for a change. You work so hard, and you have a lot of responsibility on your shoulders, so it's my job to make your home a haven." She kept her eyes on George the whole time, and when Star knew he was listening, she added, "If it's okay with you, can we have the Hammonds over again tomorrow? Maybe by then

I'll think of something special for you to do for me, since you keep asking."

"George, did you hear that? My wife enjoys your company so much she wants you to come back again tomorrow for dinner. I'm gonna have to start taking money out of your check for meals if this keeps up!" They both laughed. George was in good spirits as he left that evening thinking life was really good. He had seen Star watching him and assumed that she was admiring his good looks. After all, he had been working out lately, and he guessed the effects were starting to show. The close-fitting black turtleneck that he had chosen to wear emphasized the chiseled look he was perfecting. Watching her watch him had made him flex even more.

He decided to stop by the office on his way home to pick up some papers. Just as he came into the building, he ran into his nemesis, Marty Johnson. Marty didn't even acknowledge his presence, which irritated him to no end. George shook it off and determined not to let that flea ruin his high. He got the papers he wanted and went home. He boasted all the way home to his wife, Zora, about how much influence he had within the company and how he had such a great relationship with Xavier. George even called one of the other managers to brag about getting invited to Xavier's house for dinner and the fact that he was going back the next night. The only thing that put a damper on his mood was the fact that Marty was still a thorn in his side.

After they reached the house and started getting ready for bed, George continued talking to his wife about his frustration with Marty. "He's always second-guessing my decisions at work and basically questioning my judgment."

His wife asked him why he hadn't already fired Marty. "You're getting ready to shut down the production side anyway. Someone else can run that department for the next couple of months. Why don't you just get rid of him if he bothers you so?"

George kissed his wife. "That's a great idea. I'll make that happen tomorrow. I don't know why I didn't think of that myself! Come here and let me thank you properly. You just made my day." Zora giggled and eagerly joined him under the

covers.

Chapter 7 - Marty's Day in the Sun

That night Xavier had thanked his wife for dinner the way a man best shows his love and appreciation. She was now purring in her sleep like a satisfied cat, but he couldn't sleep, so he got up to do some work. Xavier was looking over the change-management plans for transitioning their operations work overseas and decided to review some of the key personnel files. There might be some folks he could use in other parts of the business. He picked up the file for the head of production, Martin Kyle Johnson. None of the other managers realized that Marty was Star's uncle because they had always had a professional relationship. Knowing that he would have to find something for his cousin in the reorganization, Xavier wanted to get up to speed on his prior experience. While reviewing the contents of the file, he saw the memo regarding Marty having been the one to uncover the embezzlement plot a few months back. Xavier made a note to make sure Marty was rewarded for his efforts.

The next morning, when he got to the office, he asked his assistant if any honor or recognition had been given to Marty Johnson for uncovering the plot to steal from the company.

"Nothing has been done for him. We really don't have a formal reward and recognition program in place. I can check with some of the other managers to see what types of recognition they've done in the past if you want to be consistent."

George had just gotten off the elevator and was headed to tell Xavier about his decision to fire Marty. When Xavier looked up and saw George walking toward his office, he shook his head to his assistant and said, "Don't worry about it. I'll just check with George. He knows everything that's going on in this office. Him handling the office allows me to focus on mergers and acquisitions as well as new business development. He'll deal with it."

As George entered the executive suite, Xavier asked him, "What kind of recognition should I give as CEO if I want to honor someone?"

Thinking that Xavier might be planning to honor him, George answered, "Well, if it's coming from you it should be something significant and bigger than anything we would do as department heads. I'd recommend establishing a President's Choice Award with some type of trophy or plaque that could be displayed for everyone to see with your signature on it as well as a hefty bonus check. Maybe you could even have a banquet in the person's honor. You should go all out if it's coming from the CEO."

Xavier smiled. "That's a great idea! Can you make that happen? I want to honor Marty Johnson for reporting his suspicions and uncovering that plot to embezzle from the company. Do everything you said, even the banquet. This man really saved us."

George turned and left in shock. He went through the motions of ordering the award and requesting the bonus. He even had his assistant start the planning for a banquet, but he hated every bit of it. Finally, he left the office and went home.

When he told his wife what happened, she agreed that there was nothing he could do about it.

"Since Marty has so much goodwill with the people in this town, if you say anything against him publically, you'll look bad. Worse, you'll look like a bigot because it will seem like you're just mad because he's Black. Let's just get ready to go to dinner. I'm sure you'll feel better after a few glasses of wine." Zora turned to go get ready, and George followed on her heels, realizing she was right.

~

At dinner things went from bad to worse. Star served baked brie and smoked salmon as an appetizer. For the main course she had cooked a rack of lamb with rosemary, roasted potatoes, and carrots. She even had the traditional paper frills on the rib-bone ends. Dessert was a chocolate lava cake with a molten chocolate center. His favorite! Xavier was so full he thought he might burst, and he was so proud of his wife's skills. They were drinking wine after dinner when Xavier asked Star for the third time, "Baby, you have outdone yourself.

Dinner was wonderful. Tell me what I can do for you. There has to be something you want. "

Star leaned close to Xavier and said, "Sweetie, if you really love me, if you really want to do something for me, you would spare my loved ones and me from the impact of your company moving its operations." She paused, knowing that she now had George's attention as well. "This plan to move the jobs out of the country will mean that most of the local folks in this town will lose their livelihoods including many of my family members and friends. If it was just a few layoffs or pay cuts it wouldn't be so devastating, and I would not say anything. I would never do anything to interfere with your work if I didn't think this were a life-or-death situation. But it seems this plan was put in place because of spite and hatefulness. The numbers that you were shown don't reveal the total economic impact. You stand to make a lot of money initially, but there are a lot of hidden costs with moving the work overseas. In the meantime, this city will suffer, and the severance plan that is being offered to those impacted is a mere pittance. You will look like you are benefiting from the suffering of the local workers who will lose their jobs. I know that you're not that kind of man. If you had known the total impact on the local economy, you would have considered it more carefully. Will you at least promise to review the data again? Maybe there is more to this scheme than you know."

Xavier turned to George and asked, "Is this true? What have you done? This will be a public relations nightmare if I'm seen to have taken away all the jobs from town. What was I thinking to leave this all to you?" Xavier got up in a rage and stormed out into the backyard. He realized that he'd left too much of the planning to George and hadn't spent enough time analyzing this deal. He was more upset with himself than anything, but he was glad the deal wasn't yet finalized. He would have time to review the numbers in more detail and understand the true implications.

Recognizing how much influence Star had on his boss, George fell on his knees in front of her on the couch and put his arms around her, begging for her support. When Xavier came back into the room and saw George, he exclaimed, "What? Now you're going to molest my wife in my own house? You're fired!"

Chapter 8 - A Man for the People

Later that evening Star told Xavier that her cousin Marty was the one who told her about the plans George had to get rid of all the local workers.

"I don't think George really likes Black people. Maybe that was a part of his motivation for ruining their livelihoods."

"Well that doesn't make any sense. He and I have been friends for too long. We've never had any issues and he's never said anything derogatory about Blacks or any minority group."

Xavier didn't want to believe that his college friend was trying to manipulate him. He knew George was overreaching at times and that he often put down the workers in the Production Department. Now that Star had brought it to his attention, he realized that he had been too caught up in George's plans to save them money to think about the implications for the workers.

"George is a bit elitist but I just wrote that off as a side effect of privilege. He didn't have to work hard for anything. He grew up in a wealthy suburb outside of Atlanta and his parents foot the entire bill for college. He can't really relate to people who had a different experience. Come to think of it, he's always been rather insensitive when we talk about raising wages or improving the benefits package. I just thought he was looking out for my bottom line."

Star pleaded with Xavier to rethink sending the operations jobs overseas. She asked him to discuss the plans with Marty and consider the decision more carefully. Even though it was late they invited Marty over. Together the three of them discussed how Xavier might save money on his operations budget and still keep some production in the states. He was impressed with his wife's business savvy and her ideas for restructuring some of their investments to get higher returns. Star wasn't just a pretty face.

Marty informed them that there was new technology that would streamline their production and systemize a lot of the administration activity. He said he'd been trying to convince George to invest in the technology for over a year without success. Xavier asked for a meeting with the vendor to get more information, and they came up with a plan to retrain some of the workers so that they could be redeployed to work in other parts of the company. Marty knew most of the employees and their strengths and weaknesses. He also knew which ones were planning to retire soon anyway. With his knowledge of the people and Xavier's willingness to listen to his ideas, almost all of the jobs were salvaged. There were a few casualties—but they would get to leave with dignity and a very lucrative severance package.

"You know, the last two days have been exhausting, but it's been good work," said Xavier after they finalized the new change-management plan. "I think we should commemorate these two days each year and make them company holidays in honor of the change in our company culture. We had somehow lost our sense of direction and our humanity in the name of making a profit. However, these holidays will remind us that the people are the ones who make us great. We need to develop all employees to their greatest potential and focus on training them so that they can be marketable internally or even externally if necessary. Susa Industries will be an employer of choice because word will get out that we develop our people."

Within six months, it was amazing to see how many employees actually demonstrated an aptitude for working in more areas of the company. A program was put in place that allowed employees to assess abilities in key competency areas and created a training and development plan for continuous improvement. Some employees were surprisingly even willing to relocate to other locations to get more opportunities. The plan was a win-win for everyone. It seemed that Xavier's openness to giving employees the tools they needed to succeed and the opportunities to reach beyond the production floor was a positive boost to morale. The work environment and productivity within the organization improved tenfold. Marty was promoted to chief operations officer and became a key player in the strategic-planning activities for the whole corporation.

Chapter 9 - A Good Wife

Later that year Xavier reflected on his marriage to Star and wondered how he had gotten so lucky the second time around. The last time he asked her what he could do for her, she told him that all she wanted was for him to give his life fully to Christ. He didn't want to know what life would be like without her, and he certainly didn't want to consider eternity without her. He had heard her pray often enough to know that salvation wasn't about just believing in God. It was about inviting Him into his heart and having a relationship with Him that was a priority over all others. He had finally decided to do it, and his life had changed immediately. He had a new found since of purpose and it affected his decisions at home and a work. Xavier had to give Star credit for the change in him over the last few months. She was a living testimony before him of what a life in Christ was all about. She made him want to be a better man. Star also did an excellent job taking care of Xavier. She always asked "Do you need anything?" or "Is there something I can get for you?" He offered up a prayer of thanksgiving for the partner he had found to complete his life. Then he spent some time reading the book of Ecclesiastes and felt the presence of God as he soaked up wisdom from Solomon.

Star came into his office just as he was concluding his morning meditation. Xavier was full of emotion as he said "Baby I'm so blessed to have you in my life. I was just reading in Ecclesiastes 4 that two is better than one because they can help each other up when one falls and keep each other warm. It also said that a cord of three is not easily broken which reminds me how important God is to our relationship. When a man finds a woman who honors and respects him and plays her role in supporting him in all his endeavors, he can trust her with everything. With you and God on my side, I know that I have already achieved what most men don't even know that they are missing." He pulled her into his arms and kissed her upturned smile.

"It's me who has been blessed. Who would have

thought that a silly beauty contest could actually bring two people together and it work out so well. I am so proud of you and how you demonstrate your love for God in the way that you treat me. I can't wait till our first child arrives. You're going to be a great dad."

He leaned down to place a kiss on her round belly and wondered how life could get any better. Star was the glue and the balance in his life. It was his honor to have her by his side, and she made sure that their household ran smoothly. She was charitable and industrious, but he most valued the strength and dignity that she wore like a garment. It had taken him a while to really understand what the scripture meant when it said that charm is deceitful and that beauty is fleeting. He had finally realized that what made Star a good wife was her faith—her faith in God and her faith in him.

.

Chapter 10 - Redemption

Early one Sunday morning, breakfast was on the table and Oliver Stanton, morning news anchor for WKRN in Nashville, sat down with his morning paper. He looked over at his beautiful wife and asked, "Baby what are you smiling about?"

Tiana smiled to as she put down the card and envelope she had just opened. "I just got a birth announcement from Xavier and Star Thomas. They had a precious little baby girl who they named Bella. Look at the picture. She's beautiful just like the name implies."

"That's nice sweet heart. I'm happy for them."

"Me too. Who would have believed that Xavier would have become the community leader that he is today. I read an article about him in Black Enterprise magazine this month and he spoke about his faith, his family, and his company's commitment to serving the communities in which that had a presence. His company is going public. I'm so proud of his success and I'm glad that he's got such a supportive wife."

Oliver reached across the table and took her hand. "Sorry, but I've got the prize there. You are the best wife ever. Beautiful, smart, loving…you're an amazing woman. Here you are the youngest president of the largest Black-owned bank, social activist, and regional director for your sorority, and you still make time for me."

He finally took a bite into his breakfast. "And you can cook too! The quiche you made this morning is delicious. Xavier didn't know how to love someone like you. It takes a very secure man to appreciate the beauty of partnering with someone equally ambitious and successful."

"You're biased baby, but thanks. I'm glad you like my cooking. I realized with you that marriage is what you make it. As long as too people are committed to each other, they can overcome any obstacles that life throws your way. You just have to be in it to win at it. Now hurry up and finish or we will be late for church. I'm teaching the women's Sunday school class. "

Questions for Discussion

1. What do you think led to the problems in Xavier's first marriage?

2. Is there anything wrong with two career-oriented people getting married?

3. What would it take for such a marriage to work?

4. Do you think Xavier and his first wife were in love? Is that important in marriage?

5. How do you show respect when both the man and the woman are financial equals?

6. Consider how Star/Esther won favor with Xavier in this story. How do women present themselves before men to get their attention?

7. Should a Christian consider marrying an unsaved man or woman?

8. How do women sanctify their husbands if they find themselves in that situation?

9. Do you think Star/Esther loved her husband? If not, how do you think that impacted her?

10. The Bible calls wives to respect their husbands. In what specific ways did Star/Esther show her husband respect? How was that different from his first wife, Tiana?

11. In what ways are you like Xavier?

12. In what ways are you like Star/Esther? Or Tiana?

13. What do you think of Marty putting Star in a beauty contest?

14. Do you think Xavier was a good catch? What about Star? What about Tiana?

15. In what ways did Star/Esther influence Xavier? Do you agree that she was a good wife?

Personal Reflection

How does this story relate to your life?

_____

_____

_____

_____

How is God calling you to respond to what you've read?

_____

_____

_____

_____

Message from the Author

I hope you enjoyed reading my interpretation of this story. Each of the characters was a joy to bring to life and try to get into their heads so we could understand what motivates people. The fact that Xavier considered himself a Christian with no zeal for the church is very similar to the apathy of many Jews who had been in captivity for years and stayed behind after others returned to the Promised Land. God watched over them still. Just as he watches over so many believers today who are still outside of the church. Star is the type of woman and wife I think many of us aspire to be but fall short sometimes. I always felt for Vashti in the Book of Esther and wondered what happened to her. Finally, we all need a "Marty" in our lives – a trusted spiritual advisor who can pray for us and with us as we travel along life's journey.

My entire collection of short stories based on different women in the bible will be published soon. My desire is that we can all see a bit of ourselves in "her" stories. Be sure to read them all and feel free to send me your comments. I'd love to hear from you. If you enjoyed this book, Star, please visit www.amazon.com to write a review.

Follow my blog: www.dvineinsights.blogspot.com

Contact me: divineinsightspress@gmail.com